Gordon the Big Engine

THE REV. W. AWDRY

WITH ILLUSTRATIONS BY
C. REGINALD DALBY

HEINEMANN YOUNG BOOKS

Gordon the Big Engine

Originally published in Great Britain 1953 as Book 8 in The Railway Series
First published in this new edition 1999
by Egmont Children's Books Limited
239 Kensington High Street, London, W8 6SL
Book design by Mandy Norman and Ness Wood

ISBN 0 434 80457 6

3 5 7 9 10 8 6 4

Printed in Italy

DEAR IAN,

You asked for a book about Gordon. Here it is. Gordon has been naughty, and the Fat Controller was stern with him.

Gordon has now learnt his lesson and is a Really Useful Engine again.

THE AUTHOR

Off the Rails

Gordon was resting in a siding.

"Peep peep! Peep peep! Hullo, Fatface!"
whistled Henry.

"What cheek!" spluttered Gordon. "That Henry is
too big for his wheels; fancy speaking to me like that!
Me e e e e!" he went on, letting off steam,
"Me e e e who has never had an accident!"

"Aren't jammed whistles and burst safety valves

accidents?" asked Percy innocently.

"No indeed!" said Gordon huffily, "high spirits – might happen to any engine; but to come off the rails, well I ask you! Is it right? Is it decent?"

A few days later it was Henry's turn to take the Express. Gordon watched him getting ready.

"Be careful, Henry," he said, "You're not pulling the 'Flying Kipper' now; mind you keep on the rails today."

Henry snorted away, Gordon yawned and went to sleep.

But he didn't sleep long.
"Wake up, Gordon," said his
Driver, "a Special train's
coming and we're to
pull it."

Gordon opened his eyes.
"Is it Coaches or Trucks?"
"Trucks," said his Driver.
"Trucks!" said Gordon
crossly. "Pah!"

They lit Gordon's fire and oiled him
ready for the run. The fire was sulky
and wouldn't burn; but they
couldn't wait, so Edward pushed
him to the turntable to get him
facing the right way.

"I *won't* go, I *won't* go," grumbled Gordon.

"Don't be silly, don't be silly,"
puffed Edward.

Gordon tried hard, but he couldn't stop
himself being moved.

At last he was on the turntable, Edward was
uncoupled and backed away, and Gordon's
Driver and Fireman jumped down to turn
him round.

The movement had shaken Gordon's fire; it was now burning nicely and making steam.

Gordon was cross, and didn't care what he did.

He waited till the table was half-way round. "I'll show them! I'll show them!" he hissed, and moved slowly forward.

He only meant to go a little way, just far enough to "jam" the table, and stop it turning, as he had done once before. But he couldn't stop himself, and, slithering down the embankment, he settled in a ditch.

"Oooosh!" he hissed as his wheels churned the mud. "Get me out! Get me out!"

"Not a hope," said his Driver and Fireman, "you're stuck, you silly great engine, don't you understand that?"

They telephoned the Fat Controller.

* * *

"So Gordon didn't want to take the Special and ran into a ditch," he answered from his office. "What's that you say? The Special's waiting – tell Edward to take it please – and Gordon? Oh leave him where he is; we haven't time to bother with him now."

A family of toads croaked crossly at Gordon as he lay in the mud. On the other side of the ditch some little boys were chattering.

"Coo! Doesn't he look silly!"

"They'll never get him out."

They began to sing:

Silly old Gordon fell in a ditch,
fell in a ditch,
fell in a ditch,
Silly old Gordon fell in a ditch,
All on a Monday morning.

The School bell rang
and, still singing, they
chased down the road.

"Pshaw!" said
Gordon, and blew
away three
tadpoles
and an
inquisitive newt.

Gordon lay in the ditch all day.

"Oh dear!" he thought, "I shall never get out."

But that evening they brought floodlights; then with powerful jacks they lifted Gordon and made a road of sleepers under his wheels to keep him from the mud.

Strong wire ropes were fastened to his back end, and James and Henry, pulling hard, at last managed to bring him to the rails.

Late that night Gordon crawled home a sadder and a wiser engine!

Leaves

Two men were cleaning Gordon.
"Mind my eye," Gordon grumbled.

"Shut it, silly! Did ever you see such mud, Bert?"

"No I never, Alf! You ought to be ashamed, Gordon, giving us extra work."

The hosing and scrubbing stopped. Gordon opened one eye, but shut it quickly.

"Wake up, Gordon," said the Fat Controller sternly, "and listen to me. You will pull no more coaches till you are a Really Useful Engine."

So Gordon had to spend his time pulling trucks.

"Goods trains, Goods trains," he muttered. He felt his position deeply. "That's for you! — and *you*! — *and* you!" Gordon said crossly.

"Oh! Oh! Oh! Oh!" screamed the trucks as he shunted them about the Yard.

"Trucks will be trucks," said James, watching him.

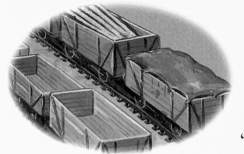

"They won't with *me*!"
snorted Gordon. "I'll teach them.
Go on!" and another truck
scurried away.

"They tried

to push me
down the hill this morning,"
Gordon explained. "It's
slippery there. You'll probably
need some help."

"*I* don't need help on hills," said James huffily.

Gordon laughed, and got ready for his next train.

James went away to take the Express.

"Slippery hills indeed," he snorted.
"*I* don't need help."

"Come on! Come on!" he puffed.

"All in good time, all in good time,
grumbled the coaches.

The train was soon running nicely, but a "Distant"
signal checked them close to Gordon's Hill.

Gordon's Hill used to be bleak and bare. Strong winds

from the sea made it hard to climb. Trees were planted to give shelter, and in summer the trains run through a leafy avenue.

Now autumn had come, and dead leaves
fell. The wind usually puffed them away,
but today rain made them heavy, and they
did not move.

The "Home" signal showed "clear", and
James began to go faster.

He started to climb the hill.

"I'll do it! I'll do it!" he puffed
confidently.

Half-way up he was not so sure!

"I *must* do it, I *must* do it," he panted desperately, but try as he would, his wheels slipped on the leaves, and he couldn't pull the train at all.

"Whatsthematter? Whatsthematter?" he gasped.

"Steady old boy, steady," soothed his Driver.

His Fireman put sand on the rails to help him grip; but

James' wheels spun so fast that they only ground the sand and leaves to slippery mud, making things worse than before.

The train slowly stopped. Then –

"Help! Help! Help!" whistled James; for though his wheels were turning forwards, the heavy coaches pulled him backwards, and the whole train started slipping down the hill.

His Driver shut off steam, carefully put on the brakes, and skilfully stopped the train.

"Whew!" he sat down and mopped his face. "I've never known *that* happen before."

"I have," said the Fireman, "in Bincombe tunnel – Southern Region."

The Guard poked his head in the cab. "Now what?" he asked.

"Back to the station," said the Fireman, taking charge, "and send for a 'Banker'."

So the Guard warned the
Signalman, and they brought
the train safely down.
But Gordon,
who had
followed
with a goods
train, saw what had happened.
Gordon left his trucks, and
crossed over to James.

"I thought you could climb hills," he chuckled.

James didn't answer; he had no steam!

"Ah well! We live and learn," said Gordon, "we live and learn. Never mind, little James," he went on kindly, "I'm going to push behind. Whistle when you're ready."

James waited till he had plenty of steam, then "Peep! Peep!" he called.

"Poop! Poop! Poop!"

"Pull hard," puffed Gordon.

"We'll do it!" puffed James.

"Pull hard! We'll do it," the engines puffed together.

Clouds of smoke and steam towered from the snorting engines as they struggled up the hill.

"We *can* do it!" puffed James.

"We *will* do it!" puffed Gordon.

The greasy rails sometimes made Gordon's wheels slip, but he never gave up, and presently they reached the top.

"We've done it! We've done it!" they puffed.

Gordon stopped. "Poop! Poop! He whistled. "Goodbye."

"Peep! Peep! Peep! Peep!
Thank you! Goodbye," answered James. Gordon watched the coaches wistfully till they were out of sight; then slowly he trundled back to his waiting trucks.

 # Down the Mine

O ne day Thomas was at the junction, when Gordon shuffled in with some trucks.

"Poof!" remarked Thomas, "what a funny smell!"

"Can you smell a smell?"

"I can't smell a smell,"
said Annie and Clarabel.

"A funny, musty sort
of smell," said Thomas.

"No one noticed it till you did," grunted Gordon. "It must be yours."

"Annie! Clarabel! Do you know what I think it is?" whispered Thomas loudly. "It's ditchwater!"

Gordon snorted, but before he could answer, Thomas
puffed quickly away.

Annie and Clarabel could hardly believe their ears!

"He's *dreadfully* rude; I feel *quite* ashamed."

"I feel quite ashamed, he's dreadfully rude," they
twittered to each other.

"You mustn't be rude, you make us ashamed," they kept telling Thomas.

But Thomas didn't care a bit.

"That was funny, that was funny," he chuckled. He felt very pleased with himself.

Annie and Clarabel were deeply shocked. They had a great respect for Gordon the Big Engine.

Thomas left the coaches at a station and went to a mine for some trucks.

Long ago, miners, digging for lead, had made tunnels under the ground.

Though strong enough to hold up trucks, their roofs could not bear the weight of engines.

A large notice said: "DANGER. ENGINES MUST NOT PASS THIS BOARD."

Thomas had often been warned, but he didn't care.

"Silly old board," he thought. He had often tried to pass it, but had never succeeded.

This morning he laughed as he puffed along. He had made a plan.

He had to push empty trucks into one siding, and pull out full ones from another.

His Driver stopped him, and the Fireman went to turn the points.

"Come on," waved the Fireman, and they started.

The Driver leaned out of the cab to see where they were going.

"Now!" said Thomas to himself, and, bumping the trucks fiercely, he jerked his Driver off the footplate.

"Hurrah!" laughed Thomas, and he followed the trucks into the siding.

"Stupid old board!" said Thomas as he passed it. "There's no danger; there's no danger."

His Driver, unhurt, jumped up. "Look out!" he shouted.

The Fireman clambered into the cab. Thomas squealed crossly as his brakes were applied.

"It's quite safe," he hissed.

"Come back," yelled the Driver, but before they could move, there was rumbling and the rails quivered.

The Fireman jumped clear. As he did so the ballast slipped away and the rails sagged and broke.

"Fire and Smoke!" said Thomas, "I'm sunk!" – and he was!

Thomas could just see out of the hole, but he couldn't move. "Oh dear!" he said, "I am a silly engine."

"And a very naughty one too," said a voice behind him, "I saw you."

"Please get me out; I won't be naughty again."

"I'm not so sure," replied the Fat Controller. "We can't lift you out with a crane, the ground's not firm enough. Hm . . . Let me see . . . I wonder if Gordon could pull you out."

"Yes Sir," said Thomas nervously. He didn't want to meet Gordon just yet!

"Down a mine is he? Ho! Ho! Ho!" laughed Gordon.

"What a joke! What a joke!" he chortled, puffing to the rescue.

"Poop! Poop! Little Thomas," he whistled, "we'll have you out in a couple of puffs."

Strong cables were fastened between the two engines.

"Poop! Poop! Poop!"

"Are you ready? HEAVE,"

called the Fat Controller.

But they didn't pull
Thomas out in two puffs;
Gordon was panting
hard and nearly purple
before he had dragged
Thomas out of the
hole, and safely past
the board.

"I'm sorry I was
cheeky," said Thomas.

"That's all right, Thomas. You made me laugh. I like that. I'm in disgrace," Gordon went on pathetically, "I feel very low."

"I'm in disgrace too," said Thomas.

"Why! so you are Thomas; we're both in disgrace. Shall we form an Alliance?"

"An Ally – what – was – it?"

"An Alliance, Thomas, 'United we stand, together we fall,'" said Gordon grandly. "You help me, and I help you. How about it?"

"Right you are," said Thomas.

"Good! That's settled," rumbled Gordon.

And buffer to buffer the Allies puffed home.

Paint Pots and Queens

The stations on the line were being painted. The engines were surprised.

"The Queen is coming," said the painters. The engines in their shed were excited and wondered who would pull the Royal Train.

"I'm too old to pull important trains," said Edward sadly.

"I'm in disgrace," Gordon said gloomily. "The Fat Controller would never choose me."

"He'll choose me, of course," boasted James the Red Engine.

"You!" Henry snorted, "*You* can't climb hills. He will ask *me* to pull it, *and* I'll have a new coat of paint. You wait and see."

The days passed. Henry puffed about proudly, quite sure that he would be the Royal Engine.

One day when it rained, his Driver and Fireman stretched a tarpaulin from the cab to the tender, to keep themselves dry.

Henry puffed into the Big Station.

A painter was climbing a ladder above the line. Henry's smoke puffed upwards; it was thick and black. The painter choked and couldn't see. He missed his footing on the ladder, dropped his paint pot, and fell plop on to Henry's tarpaulin.

The paint poured over Henry's boiler, and trickled down each side. The paint pot perched on his dome.

The painter clambered down and shook his brush at Henry.

"You spoil my clean paint with your dirty smoke," he said, "and then you take the whole lot, and make me go and fetch some more."

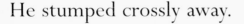

He stumped crossly away.

The Fat Controller pushed through the crowd.

"You look like an iced cake, Henry," he said.

"*That* won't do for the Royal Train. I must make other arrangements."

He walked over to the Yard.

Gordon and Thomas saw him coming, and both began
to speak.

"Please Sir ———"

"One at a time," smiled the Fat Controller. "Yes Gordon?"

"May Thomas have his branch line again?"

"Hm," said the Fat Controller,
"well Thomas?"

"Please, Sir, can Gordon
pull coaches now?"

The Fat Controller pondered.

"Hm ——— you've both

been quite good lately, and you deserve a treat ——
When the Queen comes, Edward will go in front and
clear the line, Thomas will look after the coaches, and
Gordon —— will pull the train."

"Ooooh Sir!" said the engines happily.

The great day came. Percy, Toby, Henry and James worked hard bringing people to the town.

Thomas sorted all their coaches in the Yard.

"Peep! Peep! Peep! They're coming!" Edward steamed in, looking smart with flags and bright paint.

Two minutes passed – five – seven – ten. "Poop! Poop!" Everyone knew that whistle, and a mighty cheer went up as the Queen's train glided into the station.

Gordon was spotless, and his brass shone. Like
Edward, he was decorated with flags, but on his buffer
beam he proudly carried the Royal Arms.

The Queen was met by the Fat Controller, and before doing anything else, she thanked him for their splendid run.

"Not at all, Your Majesty," he said, "thank *you*."

"We have read," said the Queen to the Fat Controller, "a great deal about your engines. May we see them please?"

So he led the way to where all the engines were waiting.

"Peep! Peep!" whistled Toby and Percy, "they're coming!"

"Sh Sh! Sh Sh!" hissed Henry and James.

But Toby and Percy were too excited to care.

The Fat Controller told the Queen their names, and she talked to each engine. Then she turned to go.

Percy bubbled over, "Three cheers for the Queen!" he called.

"Peeeep! Peeeep! Peeeep!" whistled all the engines.

The Fat Controller held his ears, but the Queen, smiling, waved to the engines till she passed the gate.

Next day the Queen spoke specially to Thomas, who fetched her coaches, and to Edward and Gordon who took her away; and no engines ever felt prouder than Thomas, and Edward, and Gordon the Big Engine.